CHRISTMAS INN
Lancaster

AUBREE VALENTINE

Christmas Inn Lancaster

Copyright ©2021 by Aubree Valentine

All rights reserved.

All rights reserved worldwide. No part of this book may be reproduced, copied or transmitted in any medium, whether electronic, internet, or otherwise, without the expressed permission of the author.

This is a work of fiction. All characters, events, locations, and names occurring in this book are the product of the author's imagination or are the property of their respective owners and are used fictitiously. Any resemblances to actual events, locations, or persons (living or dead), is entirely coincidental and not intended by the author.

All trademarks and trade names are used in a fictitious manner and are in no way endorsed by or an endorsement of their respective owners.

Contains sexual situations, violence, sensitive and offensive language and mature topics. Recommended for age 18 years and up.

Cover Design & Formatting Beyond the Bookshelf Publishing Services

Photo Credits: DepositPhotos

Also by Aubree Valentine

Too Hot to Handle Series
Hot Cop
Cop Tease
Strip Search
Cop Blocked
Covert Affair
Wild Fire
Ex-Con
Fed Up
The R&D Stables Series
Ranger
The following titles are now in Kindle Unlimited:
The Day and Knight Trio
Damon
Knight
Gigi (coming in 2023)
425 Madison Series
Love Under Construction
Love Under Protection

SUSAN STOKER'S BADGE OF HONOR WORLD
Justice for Danielle
Rescuing Harlow
Saving Sadie
MAN OF THE MONTH CLUB - SYCAMORE MOUNTAIN
Drunk Dial
CURVES FOR CHRISTMAS
Sugar Cookie Kisses
THE CHRISTMAS INN SERIES
Christmas Inn Lancaster
Christmas Inn Blue Ridge
Christmas Inn Piegon Forge
Christmas Inn St. Petersburg
THE REXFORD ROYALS SERIES
Royally F*cked
Royally Scr*wed

Author's Note:

Dear Reader,

The Christmas Inn series currently consists of five short stories featuring the Tinsley family.

They're quick reads filled with holiday magic meant to make you smile.

I hope that you enjoy each and every one of them.

Xo,
    Aubree

Dedication

This one is for my dad.

Born on Christmas Day with a love for the holidays and a mild annoyance for his baby girl who enjoyed redecorating his Christmas tree the minute he perfected it.

For my mom. Who he loved beyond measure.

And my stepdad who stepped up and has been there since my own kids took their first breaths.

Holidays are about family. And I'm damn sure thankful for the one I've got.

PROLOGUE

Mason popped the collar on his wool coat and pulled up his scarf as he hustled through the busy streets of Chicago, heading for home. Thanks to a cold front that pushed through, they were already seeing their first snowstorm of the season. Which only added to the frigid temperature this time of night. At least he wasn't dealing with the usual weekday foot traffic, just a few stragglers that were brave enough to face the weather for a date night or a few beers with friends.

Not Mason. Mason was on his way home from work and dreaming of a nice hot shower before heating up a frozen pizza and having a beer or two in front of the fireplace while some cheesy holiday movie played in the background.

Judge if you must, but he was a sucker for all those feel-good romantic Christmas movies that played over and over from what seemed like November 1st through the New Year. If asked, he'd probably deny it unless it earned him some brownie points with the right woman.

A woman who wasn't his who seemed to enjoy making fun of his movie preferences.

It had been a while since Etta crossed his mind. Burying himself in work seemed to really help distract him, and he preferred it that way. Otherwise the anger and betrayal would take over and that did him no good.

Before he could let his thoughts get too carried away, his apartment building came into view. He quickly keyed in his access code and stepped inside, shaking the snow off of his hair and shoulders in the entry before crossing the foyer to the elevator.

Already focused on the shower that was practically calling his name, he never noticed the familiar figure following him inside. The earbuds in his ears were blasting Five Finger Death Punch and tuned out all the noise that followed.

He hustled down the hall when the elevator opened on his floor and unlocked the door to his apartment, where he shed his scarf and coat, hanging them on the hooks he installed near the door. Warm air enveloped him like a cozy blanket while Mason quickly untied his work boots, set them on the shoe tray, and then headed right to the bathroom.

Clothes tossed in the hamper, and the shower water heated to the perfect temperature; Mason climbed inside and sighed as the water seemed to melt the cold away.

He had barely unthawed when loud knocking echoed through his apartment. With a resigned sigh and frustrated shake of his head, he quickly shut off the water and jumped out of the shower. Looked like his relaxing evening at home was going to have to wait.

Whoever was on the other side was undoubtedly persistent; that much was for sure.

"I'm coming, I'm coming," he yelled across the living space as he continued to secure a bath towel around his waist. Who the hell would even be stopping by his place unannounced this time of night anyway? It wasn't like he had a girlfriend or was expecting anyone else, for that matter.

The knocking continued, and the closer he got, the more he could hear what sounded a whole lot like a baby crying in the hallway.

Mason wasn't aware that any of his neighbors had babies, but it wasn't like he knew everyone very well. Fearing there may be some real emergency, and someone needed his help, he didn't even bother checking the peephole. When the door opened, he came face to face with his ex.

His ex, who was holding a screaming infant in her arms.

"Etta, what are you doing here?"

Last Mason had heard, Etta was off jet-setting around the world with an executive from the company Mason worked for. Rumor had it that they met at last year's Christmas party and had been seeing each other behind Mason's back for months. Of course, that was what he heard through the grapevine. It was hard to know exactly what happened when the woman packed all her shit and disappeared while he was at work, all without a word. He tried for weeks to get in touch with her and make sure she was okay, with absolutely no response.

Now she was standing here on his doorstep with a tiny baby in her arms.

"Here," she pushed the baby into his arms. "Take him. He's yours. I cannot do this anymore. I just can't." Etta dropped a bag at Mason's feet then kicked it inside his door. "I named him Thomas, all of his things are in there," she pointed to the bag before spinning on her heels and running for the steps.

Thomas. Mason's paternal grandfather's name. The only relative that he was remotely close to before his death only a few months prior.

"Wait. What do you mean, the baby is mine? Etta!"

Mason stepped out into the hall and debated chasing after her. It was too late. The door to the stairwell slammed shut, leaving Mason standing alone in a towel with the tiny green-eyed bundle of tears.

"Oooookay. Alright, buddy. Thomas," Mason stuttered and shuffled his way back inside the condo. "It's okay, little dude." He began making shushing sounds and bouncing on his feet. "How about you let me put some clothes on really quick, then we'll go from there?"

As far as introductions went, Mason was clearly underdressed for meeting the baby for the first time, regardless of if the kid was his or not. He didn't know a whole lot about babies, but he was damn sure of that much.

What in the hell was he going to do?

Did he call the police? And say what? *My ex stopped by and said he's mine. No, I don't know how to reach her.* He couldn't do that. What if they took Thomas from him and put him in foster care?

He couldn't let that happen, not after spending his youth in and out of the system and bouncing between families. Mason would do whatever he could to keep the little dude safe. Perhaps starting with a call to his best friend and personal lawyer was the way to go.

Dominic wasn't a family lawyer, but he was well known throughout Chicago and had to know someone that could help Mason. Plus, Dominic had two kids of his own with his husband Callen, so he knew a thing or two about babies.

Right. Call Dominic. As soon as he put some pants on.

He laid the baby in the middle of his bed. "Okay. Two seconds little man. Don't move," he warned, keeping one eye on the baby while he grabbed a pair of sweatpants and slipped them on. Then he grabbed his cell phone from the charger, all while little Thomas continued to wail in from the middle of Mason's bed.

This time when he picked the infant up, he settled Thomas on his shoulder and began patting his back while humming. The baby hiccupped then began to calm down.

"That's it, Buddy. I've got you now," Mason continued soothing him as he fired off a text to Dominic.

It took his friend all of five minutes before he was ringing Mason's phone. The loud sound startled Thomas, and the crying began all over again. Mason made a mental note to adjust the ringtone and maybe even find something a little less obnoxious than the sound of The Pretty Reckless at full blast.

"I'm almost surprised that you're not already standing outside my door," Mason chuckled, doing his best to add a little humor to the situation.

"I was at dinner with Callen, but I am on my way now. Fill me in."

"I'm not sure that you can really hear me over the crying. How long until you get here?"

"Ten minutes. Try changing his diaper and giving him a bottle. I'll see you soon," Dominic hung up the phone.

"Diaper and bottle," Mason repeated, reaching for the bag that Etta left. He sat the bag on his kitchen counter and started digging through it with one hand. "Okay, let's see what we've got in here."

Two diapers. One bottle that was ice cold and some clothes. That was it. Did Etta really leave her...*their*...child with so little? Was she hard up for cash? Is that why Etta dropped Thomas on his doorstep?

Guilt and regret shot through him.

What kind of situation was Thomas in before Etta decided she couldn't do it anymore? And why the hell didn't Etta come to him before now? Mason would never have hesitated to ensure the child was taken care of if Thomas really was his. He would have stepped up, taking full responsibility.

A thousand scenarios ran through his head while he tried his best to change Thomas' diaper. A task that felt like no small feat.

Maybe he should have tried harder to find Etta. Hired a PI or called his friend Cole down in Tallahassee to help track her down and make sure she was okay. Maybe then he wouldn't have just had an infant dropped on his doorstep.

Mason shook his head. A PI was probably a little over the top. What he needed to do was take a step back and stay in the moment. All he could focus on was the here and now.

Behind him, he heard a key slip in the lock and his front door open. Dom and Callen both walked in with bags in their hands.

"We made a quick pit stop because we thought you might not have a whole lot to work with," Callen gave Mason a reassuring smile.

Thomas was still busy screaming his head off.

Dominic set his bags on the counter then took the baby from Mason's arms. "Did you try a bottle?" Dom always had a nurturing way about him. Callen too. And they guys were kickass parents. Mason made the right call when he leaned on them for help.

"There was only one in the bag, and it was ice cold. I wasn't sure what to do with it. Not to mention I just got that diaper on him," he admitted. "Guys, what the fuck am I going to do?"

"First thing you're going to do is take a deep breath," Callen clapped him on the back before pulling a pack of bottles from one of the bags they brought and several cans of formula.

These two men were pseudo brothers to Mason. He knew no matter what, they'd have his back and be the voice of reason when he couldn't think clearly.

"Right, what he said," Dom agreed with his husband.

It felt pretty stupid, but Mason took that deep breath and tried to relax his shoulders.

"Good. Now, while Callen makes the little guy a bottle, start from the beginning. What exactly did Etta say?" Dominic asked.

"She literally shoved him in my arms. Said, *'His name is Thomas. He's yours. I can't do this anymore.'* Then she took off down the hall and was gone before I even had a minute to think," Mason said. "I started to go after her, but I was still in a towel, and well...yeah."

Dominic shook his head. "Did she leave any papers in the bag? Birth Certificate, or anything?"

Mason picked up the manila envelope off the counter. "There was this. I didn't open it yet."

Callen stuck the now warm bottle in Mason's free hand.

Dom took the envelope and traded him for the baby. "I'll take a look at it while you feed him."

"Uh, guys, I still don't know what to do with all this," Mason winced, looking down at the baby who was doing some weird thing with his mouth.

"Yeah, the little dude is hungry," Callen nodded. "Normally, you'd check the bottle temperature on your wrist, but I already did that for you. Now, just hold him a little more upright, not too much. Yes, perfect. Just like that. And put the bottle in his mouth. He knows how to do the rest."

Mason watched in amazement as Thomas began to suck on the bottle. His tears stopped, and he completely calmed down.

"Shit, man," Dom ran a hand over his face and sighed. "All his legal documents are here. Along with a notarized letter saying that she's left him in your care and giving you permission to seek medical treatment and make decisions in her absence."

"Is that a good thing?" Mason hesitated to ask, but he needed to know.

"Again, not my area of expertise, but it buys you a little bit of time and keeps Thomas safe in the meantime."

"Do I need to call the police?" The pit in Mason's stomach grew.

"Because she's claiming the baby is yours, I think you're within your rights to assume parentage until we get a DNA test. I'm going to phone my buddy Victor really quick. In the meantime, you might want to burp him," Dom nodded. "Then you can see if he'll take the rest of that bottle."

"I hate to be the one to say it, but Mason – you've also got to prepare yourself for the fact that Thomas may not be yours. I know I sound like an asshole right now; I just don't want to see you getting attached and having your heartbroken if he's not." Callen added.

Dom shot his husband a glare but agreed with him.

"Yeah. They say Etta wasn't a saint while we were together. What the hell do I know, right?" Even taking in their advice, Mason knew he was already attached. He was fucked no matter which way things went.

CHAPTER 2

Nestled in the heart of Lancaster County, alongside Amish farms and rich countryside – The Christmas Inn's third location was about to embark on its second holiday season.

A college graduation gift from her grandparents, Garland and Debby Tinsley, The Christmas Inn – Lancaster ran on year-round Christmas cheer and traditions that included the annual Twelve Days of Christmas festival.

Which meant the list of to-dos before the festival continued to grow, and the amount of time left to get it done was dwindling.

Shae's stress level was at an all-time high. Especially now that her groundskeeper quit suddenly. She may have understood and completely supported Fletcher's decision, but now she was in quite the bind. The groundskeeper was an integral piece of The Christmas Inn. They helped with all the decorating and were responsible for maintenance around the place. She couldn't host a fully booked Inn with no one on hand to assist in the event that something went haywire.

Now she had less than thirty days to find someone *and* get them up to speed. All while hoping that their first holiday season on board at The Christmas Inn didn't send them running for the hills. The last year had been steady, but given the number of reservations and The Christmas

Inn's overall history as a brand, Shae knew firsthand that November through March had a tendency to be nonstop.

Maybe her Assistant Manager and best friend since birth, Quinn, was on to something when she suggested Shae actually hire a few more employees overall, especially with her expansion plans for the next year. But Shae wasn't quite there yet. The issue really rested with Shae and her need to make sure things were perfect. There was still a whole slew of tasks that she refused to delegate, something that Quinn loved to point out to Shae every chance she got.

Right now, that meant one more thing on her list of things to do.

Pushing all of her other tasks to the side, for now, Shae shook the mouse on her laptop and quickly pulled up a few of the job sites she preferred to work with, as well as the local classified ads. Finding the original job listing from before the Inn opened, Shae reviewed everything and updated what she needed to before republishing the listings across all of the platforms, including the Inn's social media.

Now all she could do was wait. And perhaps work on a backup plan if she couldn't fill the spot by December 1st at the latest.

She could give her sister Nicole a call or even reach out to her cousin Meredith. They may have someone at their places that could help for a bit.

That's right. The Christmas Inn didn't just exist in Lancaster. There would one day be a grand total of at least *five* locations across the United States, including the original that was now run mostly by Meredith. Her grandparents invested in the properties and gifted each of their grandkids their own part of the family legacy.

After years of traveling back to Pigeon Forge, Tennessee and the original Christmas Inn for the holidays, Pappy and

Nana both insisted they wanted their grandkids to have their own slice of holiday cheer in a place where they wanted to put down roots. Business was booming and they had plenty of inheritance for their children, growing the franchise would lead to generational wealth for years to come if it all worked out.

As each grandchild graduated college, they were given the chance to decide where they wanted to see the next location.

For Shae, that was in the very same town she grew up in. The town where her parents still lived, just miles away. Her sister, Nicole, chose the Blue Ridge Mountains in Georgia where she graduated from college. Meredith traded her very own Inn for taking over and expanding where Nana and Pappy started it all.

Where her cousins Kane and Emberly would settle down had yet to be seen.

Shae looked up at the ceiling and sent a silent prayer to the powers that be, hoping that she would be able to find someone to dive right in. "It would really help me out if the perfect candidate somehow landed in my inbox in the next twenty-four hours," she added out loud.

The Christmas Inn was so much more than a business, The Christmas Inn brand and each of its locations served as a way to honor their grandparents. Each of their employees were more like family, like Quinn, for example, who was as close to Shae as her own flesh and blood.

There was also that pesky little rumor about a dose of Christmas Magic in the air, something Shae chose to ignore when she broke ground on The Christmas Inn – Lancaster.

That's right, the original Christmas Inn dated back decades and was the place that her great grandparents met - and fell in love. As well as her grandparents, her parents *and* each of her aunts and uncles. There was an entire tale of how each couple somehow ended up in the same place at the same time only to fall in love and live happily ever after.

Take Shae's parents for example. Her father, Nicholas Tinsley, was a ski instructor for The Christmas Inn that his parents owned. One winter, a young woman from Lancaster was vacationing with her family at The Christmas Inn and just so happened to quite literally run straight into Nicholas on the ski slope. That woman was Joy, Shae's mom.

Joy broke her arm when they both toppled over and Nicholas felt so bad that he spent the rest of the week checking in on her and bringing her sweet treats from the cafe. They shared their first kiss at midnight on New Year's and even though they were both only eighteen, they claimed that at that exact moment, they saw what their future would look like.

Right down to two girls, a dog and a farm. Her parents being the only Tinsley's that did not go into the Tinsley family business, instead they took over Joy's parents' farm and Shae's mother had a bustling quilting business of her own. All with full support from Garland and Debby Tinsley.

Pappy and Nana Tinsley never pressured any of their kids or grandkids about their futures or insisted they had to expand the family franchise. Instead, they let the "magic" do all the work as they put it.

Shae had three more sets of Aunts and Uncles as well who all claimed they were subject to Christmas Magic too. As for Shae, she may have jumped into the family business head first but she wasn't buying into the whole notion of fate, love at first sight, or magic of any kind.

Even if she was watching it happen to guests and her employees too.

True love was not for Shae Tinsley. Of this she was certain.

"Knock, knock," Quinn poked her head inside Shae's office. "Time for that staff meeting, Boss."

Shae raised a brown then rolled her eyes. "If you don't stop calling me Boss."

"Would you prefer…Bitch, instead?" Quinn teased.

There wasn't a bitchy bone in Shae's body. Usually.

But her best friend loved to give her a hard time.

"More like Boss Bitch," Shae laughed.

"Come on. I sent Isla for a coffee run and made sure she grabbed your favorite."

Oh, Quinn sure knew how to improve Shae's mood. "You need a raise."

Quinn shook her head, "You already pay me too much. Not that I'm complaining."

Shae grabbed her laptop and notepad then followed Quinn to the dining room where they were having their staff meeting today.

Her kitchen staff which consisted of her chef, Madison, and a hostess of sorts, Bianca, prepared a lunch of everyone's favorite sandwiches, pasta salad, and mini dessert cakes. As usual, the ladies knocked it out of the park, and their bonuses would reflect that. That's what this meeting was all about.

Pappy and Nana Tinsley always believed in not waiting until December to hand out bonuses, another business practice that Shae adopted as her own.

"Madison and Bianca, thank you so much for preparing lunch today. And Isla – thank you for taking the time out of your day to pick up my favorite coffee from Starbucks," Shae smiled at the three ladies chatting amongst themselves.

Bianca and Madison made great coffee in-house, but Shae still had an addiction to her favorite blend and all the extras from her favorite coffee chain. When she couldn't leave "work," Shae preferred hot tea or even hot cocoa made with Hershey's chocolate, of course.

"Oh, you're welcome, Shae," Madison waved a hand in the air. "It was nothing."

"Always happy to help," Isla added.

The only person missing was Fletcher, who wouldn't be coming back thanks to his wife's recent diagnosis. Proof that there was no way the Inn's "magic" was real. Otherwise, Fletcher wouldn't be about to lose the love of his life.

Regardless, Shae had already decided that his bonus would be hand-delivered within the next few days.

"I let our guests know that we would all be unavailable for the next thirty minutes. They have your phone number if it's an emergency and the front door is locked," Quinn reported.

The Inn didn't get a lot of random foot traffic, but occasionally a tourist would stop in to check the place out or gather information. With everyone in the dining room, Shae was glad Quinn locked up.

"Thanks, Quinn. I think we can go ahead and get started then."

CHAPTER 3

Mason scrolled through the job listings on his laptop again.

It was 2 am, and he really should be sleeping. Wasn't that what all the parenting books said anyway? *Sleep when the baby sleeps.*

In the last few weeks, he read at least a dozen of them in his very limited spare time.

There was just one small problem. He couldn't sleep. Not at 2 am after a feeding. Not at 9 pm after a bath and bottle. For the baby, not Mason, though the thought of a nice hot bath and a beer was tempting sometimes.

Maybe that's what it was. He was losing his mind. All the sleepless nights and worrying over a newborn were finally getting to him. Most days, he had to pinch himself because he still couldn't wrap his head around the fact that he had a son.

Turned out that Etta told him the truth; Thomas was his. And she wanted nothing to do with either of them. The family lawyer that Dom set Mason up with pulled quite a few strings and expedited everything, cutting all ties with Etta and making sure that Thomas would forever be safe in Mason's care.

That was the only explanation for why he was looking for a job all the way on the other side of the country in the wee hours of the morning while baby Thomas slept soundly in his bassinet beside the bed.

How in the hell a job like this one, in Pennsylvania of all places; even ended up in his search to begin with was something he couldn't figure out. As for actually considering it? Well, he chalked that up to having a baby dropped on his doorstep by a woman he thought he was in love with. Something like that tended to make a man second guess everything he once believed in. Which was precisely why within the last ten minutes he had somehow convinced himself that he needed to raise his son somewhere far away from the hustle and bustle of Chicago and the constant reminders of a mother who abandoned him.

A restless feeling had been stirring inside Mason from the moment he locked eyes with his *son*. At first, he chalked it up to coming to terms with the fact that he was a parent.

For Mason, there was no time to prepare. No adjustment period. Confused and terrified, he felt like he had only one choice. Become a parent. Not just any parent, though, but the father that Thomas Mason Carmichael deserved. The parent that Mason never had.

It didn't help that Christmas was only two weeks away, and his schedule wouldn't be letting up. Hell, his boss even asked him to be available to work on Christmas Day. His son's first Christmas and Mason would have to leave Thomas with a sitter if he didn't find a new job soon.

His son deserved a father who was present, not tied down by long hours in corporate America.

That was exactly why he was still staring at the job listing.

It was for a job that wasn't even on his radar but somehow appeared in his job search notifications a few hours ago.

The Christmas Inn - Lancaster, PA

Growing Bed & Breakfast franchise is looking for a dedicated groundskeeper and maintenance person to maintain property both inside and out at their location in the Lancaster, Pennsylvania, countryside.

The ideal candidate will be responsible for routine maintenance of the buildings, including outsourcing projects or repairs as needed. Maintaining landscape, including snow removal. Overseeing future expansion projects.

Compensation includes room and board on-site as well as a fair wage, paid time off, and other amenities.

This is a vacancy that needs to be filled immediately.

The Christmas Inn...

The name sounded familiar and caught his attention almost immediately when he was scrolling along.

Mason ran a hand over his face then opened a new tab to search for more information on this "growing franchise." The first search result linked to the official website boasting *Christmas charm all year long.* It seemed like a whimsical fairy tale, and every photo seemed to support that theory. The concept was intriguing, and each resort had its own take on the whole Christmas thing.

Christmas. Twenty-four, seven. Three hundred and sixty-five days a year.

Holidays were never a big deal when Mason was growing up, especially being passed between foster families. Could he handle that much holiday cheer?

The job did include room *and* board, plus a salary, and it didn't say anything about needing an around-the-clock dose of Christmas spirit; in fact, it mentioned *paid time off* and *vacations highly encouraged!*

Mason looked over at his son who smiled in his sleep.

He could think of worse places to raise a child. Besides, didn't most kids love a little Christmas magic?

He reread the job listing and felt that same tug to take the leap. Sure, they may think that he was overqualified but there was also a chance that he would be exactly what they were looking for.

To apply, email your resume to: tinsley.shae @ thechristmasinn . com

He checked their website one more time for good measure. The Christmas Inn currently had locations in: Tennessee, Pennsylvania, Georgia and even one just outside of Chicago – in Aurora. The Pennsylvania location was the only one with openings. Wasn't that enough of a sign to convince him?

He wanted a fresh start, and here it was. Lancaster was a cute little town that he remembered visiting once as a child. What if their future was on the East Coast? Perhaps that's where they were meant to settle down and be a family. And maybe, just maybe, Mason would even find someone that would love both of them for the rest of her life.

He could *almost* picture it.

Giving in to the sense of urgency that seemed to tingle in his bones, Mason pulled up his email and typed in the address along with a brief message before attaching his resume and cover letter. If this was really meant to be, he would know soon enough.

Not even twenty-four hours had passed before Mason received a reply back from The Christmas Inn. A woman by the name of Quinn emailed him with a few questions to be sure that he was really interested in trading his current job for something a lot more low-key and with a considerable reduction in salary. Not that The Christmas Inn didn't pay well – it simply was below Mason's current paygrade.

With the money he saved over the years, a few smart investments, and his plan to sublet his apartment in Chicago for the time being, he wasn't worried about making less money. Money meant nothing if it came at the cost of missing out on time with Thomas.

The job at The Christmas Inn sounded like a much better use of his time.

Hitting the reply button, he answered all of Quinn's questions and countered with a few of his own. Before his second cup of coffee she scheduled him for an interview during his lunch break.

From the confines of his truck he took the video call that would inevitably change his life.

Pleased with how the interview went, Mason focused on getting through the rest of the work day with a little more pep in his step than he had in a long time.

He crawled into bed that night with an answer from Quinn.

He was moving to Lancaster.

Which meant first thing the next morning he would need to stop by HR and put in his notice. A notice that was going to include using up some of that vacation time that his manager refused to approve over the years.

It was past time that Mason took a break. Even if that break would be spent packing up all his things and listing his apartment. If he had it his way, he would have everything packed up, and the two of them would be on their way to Lancaster in the next two weeks, if not sooner.

After all, what better way to celebrate Thomas first Christmas than at a place like The Christmas Inn.

CHAPTER 4

"I've been thinking," Quinn dramatically flopped down in the red velvet armchair in front of Shae's desk.

Shae groaned internally. Quinn's ideas tended to go one of two ways. It was either a brilliant idea or an insanely horrible idea. Judging by the scheming look on Quinn's face, it was probably the latter of the two this time.

"Let's hear it."

It was after check-in on Friday afternoon, which meant that things were relatively quiet. Quiet and Quinn did not go hand in hand.

"Clay and I are going to The Taproom tomorrow night with some of his friends. You should come with us," Quinn said as she popped a Hershey's Kiss in her mouth.

Yeah. Shae knew how this worked. "I'll pass but thank you. I've got a few errands to run tomorrow night, and then I plan to spend the rest of the evening relaxing at my place."

"Riiiight. Come on, Shae. When was the last time you were out on a date?"

College if she was being honest. She wasn't going to tell Quinn that, though she suspected her bestie already knew the answer.

"Who says I need to date? I'm content with the way my life is right now," Shae defended. And that was the truth. Mostly.

"You can't blame me for trying."

Quinn was right; she couldn't blame her. Now that Quinn had fallen in love (with one of their vendors at that), she wanted that kind of happiness for everyone around her. And it seemed like Quinn's matchmaking skills worked on some folks.

In fact, they had a wedding booked for Valentine's Day for a couple who met at the Single Mingle Jingle that Quinn ironically came up with as an annual event *last* Valentine's Day.

And her whole family swore it was just the Christmas Magic.

Still, it was all the more reason for Shae to avoid Quinn's setup.

Shae didn't have time for dating right now. The Christmas Inn was her significant other and would be for the foreseeable future while she continued to grow the place to fit her vision. She accepted that for what it was worth and appreciated what she had.

"What if I promise not to introduce you to any of Clay's friends?" Quinn pleaded. "When was the last time *we* went out together and had some fun?"

She arched her brow. "Because *that* wouldn't be awkward at all." Spending an evening out on the town with Quinn and Clay plus Clay's friends – without introductions? That wouldn't be weird.

"Psh. I can make things not awkward."

"Yeah, by introducing me to every one of Clay's single friends," Shae laughed.

"Come on. One night. That's all I'm asking for. Besides, your new hire should be arriving in the next twenty-four to forty-eight hours, and then you're going to be swamped with getting Mason up to speed. You deserve to cut loose once in a while."

The last time Shae cut loose, she woke up with the worst hangover and a stranger in her bed. She fought back the sly smile playing on her lips. She did have a good time, hangover aside. The stranger, who later said his name was Owen, did know a thing or two about pleasing a woman. Something her college boyfriend certainly did not.

"I see that look, Shae. You know you want to."

Quinn drove a hard bargain. But even if Shae wanted to say yes – she couldn't. There was way too much on her plate right now. The job listing she posted before Thanksgiving sat unanswered up until two weeks ago. Which meant Shae was not only doing her job but helping the other ladies fill the vacant groundskeeper position. Sure, she had help, but that didn't mean some things hadn't fallen behind.

The reminder that her new groundskeeper would be arriving soon lifted some of the weight off her shoulders and was even more reason for her to grind to catch up. That way, she could get Mason oriented to his role at The Christmas Inn – and survive the holiday.

"I'm going to have to decline. Christmas is in four days. Besides, you said so yourself, Mason will be arriving at some point this weekend, *and* we may or may not get hit by a massive snowstorm. I need to be *here*. Maybe next time."

Her best friend sighed dramatically. "Fiiiiine. Next time you can't say no."

"I didn't say no. I said maybe," Shae teased.

"Nope. Unacceptable." The phone began to ring, causing Quinn to hop up from her seat. "Isla is at lunch, so I better get that."

Shae was thankful for the reprieve even if she knew her best friend meant well.

An alert from her cell phone grabbed her attention. Her

weather app blinked on the screen. The latest predictions were showing that this snowstorm really was going to hit them.

If that was the case, she had a list of things that she needed to check on.

Grabbing a notepad and the "snow plan" folder from her file cabinet, Shae set off to make her rounds and check in with her staff.

Isla was rushing back in the door from her lunch break as Shae stepped into the front desk/seating area.

"Hey, Shae! I heard on the radio that the weather has taken a turn. I'm going to make sure all the vacant rooms are stocked with extra blankets and linens. I'll package up extras for our already occupied rooms and then deliver them after," Isla said, already on top of her prep responsibilities.

The snow could always amount to nothing, but it was best to be overly prepared.

"That would be great," Shae thanked her.

"Guess that means I should make some phone calls to our pending arrivals to make sure they're aware of the arrival of snow. I'll check on any other supplies we might need after that," Quinn told her.

"Perfect. I'm going to check in with B and Madi," Shae said while checking off items on her list.

The ladies were in the kitchen working on their dinner menu for the evening but paused to greet Shae when she walked in.

Bianca and Madison assured her that the kitchen was fully stocked with everything they may possibly need to accommodate their guests this weekend and well into next week. After putting her mind at ease about their pantry supplies, Madison handed her two cups of hot chocolate and ushered Shae onto her next stop – the barn.

The Christmas Inn was currently co-leasing some farmland adjacent to the Inn's property with an Amish family who owned horses. The young family contracted with Shae for trail rides as well as some Amish buggy rides that her guests loved.

In turn, Shae also helped cover the cost of feed and care. She had big plans for the barn, which included a few more animals – with her neighbors' help and blessing, of course. For Shae, it was important that The Christmas Inn leaned into its location and the Dutch and Amish traditions of its community.

Jeremiah was loading a wheelbarrow with firewood as she approached.

"Hi, Jeremiah. The ladies sent me with some hot cocoa for you," she smiled and held out one of the paper cups.

"Good to see you, Shae. Please tell the ladies thank you," he reached for the cup she offered then took a sip. "Miss Bianca and Miss Madison sure make good hot chocolate."

"That they do," Shae agreed. "I wanted to check in and make sure you're all set for this pending storm. If it does as predicted, it seems we're going to be hit pretty hard."

"Ah, yes. We're prepared. I was just collecting this firewood to bring up to the guest house for ya."

"Oh. Well, thank you. Be sure to let me know how much I owe you for the wood. And for your hard work too."

"It's nothing. Neighbors helping neighbors," Jeremiah shrugged.

"How's Margaret doing?" Shae asked.

Jeremiah's wife was expecting their first child soon. "She's doing well. Resting when she can. Today she's making all sorts of baked goods for the market tomorrow. Told me to come inside before I bring this wood over because she's got some goodies for you and this weekend's guests," he added.

"Oh, that would be wonderful. I'm heading to town for some things this evening. Can I bring anything back for the two of you?"

"I think we're set but thank you. Can we bring you back anything from the market tomorrow?"

"Could I trouble you for some fresh fruit and bacon?" Shae knew that Jeremiah's parents owned the produce stall, and his in-laws owned the butcher's rack. There wasn't much that she needed, but she liked to always pick up a few things when she could to support the locals.

"Ya. I'll stop by when we get home from the market and drop it off if that'll be al 'right."

"I should be around." Her home, the small carriage house that was once lived in by one of the property's previous owner's housekeepers, sat on the same piece of land that the main B&B – a ten-bedroom farmhouse portion did. Even if it was the weekend, she still made it a priority to stop by and mingle with her guests (and do a little work). Shae reached in her pocket and pulled out a few bills. "This should be enough. If it's more, promise you'll let me know."

"Yes, ma'am," he nodded, though Shae doubted he would say it cost more, even if it did.

"Thank you, Jeremiah. I'll see you soon?"

"I should be finished here in a few minutes."

"Sounds good," she said with a smile before heading back to the guest house.

It was nice to know everything was taken care of.

Once Jeremiah dropped off the firewood, Shae clocked out a few minutes ahead of schedule to hit the grocery store.

Unfortunately, her plans of beating the crowd at the store didn't go as well. The place was packed with people just like her, all rushing to grab any last-minute items they might need before the storm hit.

Shae couldn't blame them and imagined things would only get worse as more people heard the weather reports and found their way home from work. If her new hire, Mason, arrived tonight – he wouldn't have much time or options to choose from if he needed anything.

She wasn't about to let that happen. So, while she picked up things for her own place, she made sure to grab a few extras to drop off at the second carriage house that would now be Mason's.

While the usual toilet paper, bread, and milk topped her list Shae picked up some snack items too. Oatmeal (both plain and flavored), hot chocolate mix, cereal, and a few frozen dinners. She could always walk a few home cooked meals across the driveway for him too. It may not have been ideal, but at least Mason wouldn't go hungry.

Her shopping cart finally filled with everything Shae considered a necessity, she headed for the check-out line. She made friendly small talk with the cashier while the young man rang up and bagged her items. Groceries paid for, she made her way out of the store and back to her car only to discover that the forecasters were off on the start of this storm. Large snowflakes were already falling and had made a light dusting on parts of the cement as well as the cars in the parking lot. Wanting to get back to the Inn before the snowfall got heavier, Shae quickly loaded everything into her SUV and put the cart back in the cart return.

By the time she pulled up in front of her place, the snow was already falling faster. The temperature had dropped, and the roads were growing slicker. If it kept up, there was a good chance they would have a white Christmas after all.

CHAPTER 5

Mason took his time driving down the snow-covered driveway. Over the last two hours of his drive, he watched the snowfall slowly accumulate. There was easily a solid four inches covering the unplowed driveway here.

This place – his new home and "office" was something to see for the first time. The pictures on the website didn't do the place justice at all.

White Christmas lights, green garland, and wreaths with red ribbons lined the wooden fences on both sides of the driveway, welcoming weary travelers from the road and peacefully blending into the farmland surrounding it. There was nothing over the top flashy about it.

The end of the driveway opened up to a large farmhouse with an expansive front porch that ran the entire length of the home. More Christmas lights and garland decorated the porch posts, windows, and entryway. White rocking chairs with red and black plaid pillows moved slightly in the frosty wind.

Mason followed the sign to the left and into a small guest parking lot. Pulling into one of the only empty spots, he shut off his truck and looked in the backseat at Thomas, who was sound asleep.

He wasn't sure what to expect on the long drive with an infant, but he tried to be prepared, splitting the roughly ten-hour trip into two days and staying at a hotel to rest around the halfway mark. Mason didn't hesitate to stop frequently either to give Thomas a bottle, a fresh diaper, or a break from the car seat. In return, the baby handled the trip like a champ.

Now he only hoped that his son would tolerate their first night in their new home as well.

Ready to get out of the truck and get settled but not ready to wake up Thomas, Mason sighed. With the temperature continuing to drop and night quickly falling, he had no choice.

Taking off his seatbelt, he slipped his keys in his pocket, opened his door, and hopped out of the truck. The minute he opened the backdoor, Thomas' eyes opened and he looked up at Mason.

"Hey, Little Man. We made it," he cooed at his son while he unclicked his car seat. "Let's go let these nice people know we're here and see where we'll be staying."

Mason grabbed the thick baby blanket off the backseat and covered Thomas' body with it before quickly and carefully making his way across the parking lot to the front door of The Christmas Inn. The door was unlocked, and a bell jingled over his head as he walked inside. As promised, there was a blonde woman waiting for him behind the counter.

The minute the bell rang, she looked up at him with a welcoming smile that nearly had Mason fumbling over his own two feet. He didn't believe in love at first sight, but she was something to behold.

"Hi there. Welcome to Christmas Inn. Do you have a reservation with us?" The woman's voice trailed off ever so slightly at the end.

He sat Thomas' car seat on the ground and shook his head, "I'm Mason Carmichael. I spoke with Quinn about a half hour ago to let her know I would be here soon. She said Shae would be waiting for me. I'm taking it, you're Shae?" He did his best not to wince at the touch of nervousness in his voice.

Why the hell was he suddenly so out of sorts? It must have been the long car ride.

The blonde blinked twice then shook her head. "Right. Mason," she held out her hand. "I'm Shae. My apologies. It's nice to meet you."

Placing his hand in hers, Mason hissed from the contact. A spark, surely from static electricity, zapped his skin.

"Sorry," they both mumbled, then laughed at the same time.

Shae stepped around the front of the desk and kneeled down to look at Thomas. "And who is this handsome little guy? I didn't realize you had a wife and a child."

Mason cleared his throat. "No. There's no wife or anything like that. Just me and Thomas," he said as he picked the car seat up again. "I hope that's not a problem."

He sincerely hoped he didn't just pack up everything he wanted to bring with him and move across the country only to be fired before he even got started. All because he was a single dad.

"I can promise you that I'm fully committed to this job and know how to balance work and being a parent," he quickly defended.

"What?" Shae's gaze snapped back to his. "Oh, Mason, I'm so sorry. I didn't mean to make you think there was an issue. I just assumed when my assistant manager told me about you that...well, it doesn't matter what I assumed. You know what they say. Making assumptions makes people look like an ass. This little guy is no problem at all."

Mason breathed a sigh of relief. "Okay. Great. I'm sorry about getting in so late this evening. Once the snow started, traffic got a little hectic. We were so close that I didn't want to stop if I could push through."

"Makes total sense. How about I show you to your living space so you can get settled?"

"That sounds great," Mason said with a nod.

Shae reached over the counter and picked up a set of keys. "These are yours. Give me just a second to grab my coat, and I'll show you to your living space."

While Shae retrieved her coat, Mason looked around the room. There was a fireplace along one wall with stockings hung on the mantle. A Christmas tree in the corner, decorated in red and black with classic red trucks and Amish horse and buggies as ornaments. If not for the welcome desk, the place looked more like someone's private living room, right down to the inviting sofa with decorative pillows and a cozy throw draped over the back.

He was already beginning to see why this place seemed so popular among their guests.

On the opposite side of the room, there was a hallway and a staircase that was decorated with more garland, ribbons, and lights. Instead of all of the holiday cheer feeling like too much, it felt like...*home.*

The pictures on the website did not do justice to the real thing.

"Okay. Ready." Shae smiled, making his heart skip a beat once more.

This time there was a tiny hitch in his breath. It was clear, this woman could knock him flat on his ass. But that wasn't happening. Mason didn't mix business and pleasure, and he damn well wasn't going to fuck his boss.

Together they walked out the front door of the Inn,

pausing for only a moment so Shae could lock up behind her. When she turned back around, she took one look at the snow-covered parking lot and cursed under her breath.

"Everything okay?" Mason asked.

"I walked over from my place. Not thinking about the amount of snow on the ground," she laughed. "It stopped briefly before I came over here. I clearly was wrong in thinking it wouldn't start falling again so quickly."

"You can ride with us," he offered without hesitation. "Once you show me where we'll be staying, I can drop you at your place."

"I'd appreciate that. You won't need to drop me at my place. We're neighbors."

Shae carefully followed Mason across the parking lot to his truck, praying she didn't slip in the snow.

He opened the passenger side door for her and helped her in with one hand, then closed the door behind her. She waited patiently while he got Thomas settled in the back seat, paying close attention to how endearing he was with the boy. Shae didn't know Mason's story, but it was almost like he was built for fatherhood.

Once Thomas was safe and secure in the back seat, Mason hopped in the driver's seat and fired the truck up.

"All right, where to?" Mason asked as he backed the truck out of its parking space.

Shae directed him around the snow-covered road that led past the opposite side of the Inn and down a shorter driveway that ran to where both carriage houses sat.

"This one on the right is yours," she pointed to the stone carriage house on the right side of the road with a wreath hanging on each window, and a candle lit on the windowsill. "The one on the left is me. There's a parking pad on the right-hand side where you can park. Usually, it would be cleaned off."

"Got it." Mason pulled the truck into what he hoped was the concrete space and not grass or dirt. The first day at the new place and tearing up the landscaping didn't seem like the best way to make an impression.

"Why don't I help you take whatever you need inside? Then I'll leave you to it. We can meet up tomorrow sometime in my office, and I'll have you go over your paperwork and sign all your forms and stuff. I think everything else can wait until after Christmas." With only a few more days until the holiday and Mason's official start day not until the 26th, there was no sense in throwing the man into the fire yet.

"I don't have much that needs to go in tonight. A suitcase and Thomas' playpen are really all I need. Then, I'll probably head back to town and see if I can find an open store to grab a few things for the morning."

"Oh. Uhm. Well, I can carry Thomas in, and you can grab the other two things."

Mason nodded and handed her back the keys. "If you could do that, it would be amazing."

Once he got the baby carrier out of the truck, he handed Thomas off to Shae and unloaded the suitcase and playpen while she went ahead and unlocked the place.

The moment he crossed the threshold into the living room, Mason was hit with an overwhelming sense of coming home. It was unexpected but not unwelcome. He also didn't feel the least bit surprised that much like the Inn, his place was decorated for the holiday as well, including a tree with lights and a few ornaments.

Shae sat Thomas' carrier on the couch but kept one hip against it, just in case. Then she played with the zipper on her coat, nervously. "I wanted to make sure you felt welcome and wasn't sure if you had a tree of your own or not, so I put that one up. Of course, you're free to decorate it however you'd like. It doesn't have to stay up year-round either," she offered in explanation. "You could if you wanted to, but it's not mandatory or anything."

Mason nodded as he sat down his things and kicked off his snow-covered shoes. "It's nice and appreciated. Thank you. This whole place...it's something to see, that's for sure."

He saw the way Shae seemed to fill with pride, but she kept going on with her overview of the place. "There are two bedrooms upstairs. Clean sheets on both beds and clean towels in the bathroom. You mentioned you might need to go to the store. I was out earlier and picked up some things for you. I'm not sure if that will save you the trip or not, but it's all in the kitchen, on the counter. If you want to take a look before you head out. I can give you directions to the closest grocery store and big box store. The grocery store may already be closed because of the snow," Shae rambled on, unable to help herself. Nervousness fluttered through her body.

"Whoa. You did all of that?" he asked as he moved in to unbuckle his little man and get him out of the car seat.

Shae took a step back and watched him.

With Thomas cooing in his arms, he turned back around to face her. "Say, 'Thank you, Ms. Shae,'" he waved Thomas' little hand in the air and kissed his cheek.

Shae's heart swelled.

"He really is adorable." And clearly resembled his father that much was for sure. "But uhm, just Shae. No need to call me Miss." A rogue giggle bubbled out of her.

"Thanks. I'm lucky to have him. He's a good baby,

aren't you, buddy?" Mason kissed the baby again. This time the little one seemed babbled back at his father.

"If you don't need anything else, I'll let you go. My cell phone number is on the fridge. You can call or text if you need anything." Shae needed to get out of there, fast. Spending too much time watching this man with his son was not going to be good for her.

"I think we're all set. Thanks for everything, Shae. What time tomorrow should I meet you at the office?"

"I'll be around most of the day. Anytime is fine," she said, one foot already out the door.

"Okay. I'll see you then."

Shae nodded, then hurried her way out the door and across the drive to her place while Mason watched until he saw her safely inside.

"Welp, welcome home little man. What do you say we check out what's in the kitchen and get you a bottle?"

Thomas smacked his little lips and babbled.

They hadn't been here long, but Mason was already sure he'd made the right choice.

CHAPTER 6

After welcoming Mason to The Christmas Inn and running out of his place like her pants were on fire, Shae did her best to try to sleep. There was just one...or two...problems. Visions of the oh so handsome single father and his adorable son kept floating through her head.

She trusted Quinn to handle hiring Mason but all too quickly realized there was a whole lot that her best friend/assistant very conveniently forgot to mention to her. Like the fact that the man looked like sex on a stick.

Quinn also neglected to tell Shae that he was a single dad, a trait that not only made him sexier but also had Shae praying that things would work out and she wouldn't be right where she started a few weeks ago.

Shae could do a lot of things, but those things mainly happened to be behind a desk or in the kitchen. Her manual labor skills were severely limited.

It was too late to go back now, and besides that, Shae couldn't very well fire the man just because he had a baby. Not that she wanted to.

Not in the least. She meant what she said when she told Mason it wasn't an issue.

The bigger issue was her libido that suddenly woke up had her wanting to press her lips against his and finding out if his five o'clock shadow would scratch along her cheeks.

And then there was her heart, longing to cuddle his baby against her chest while rocking sweet Thomas back and forth or curling up by the fire and reading bedtime stories to him.

Even though she was always the one to balk at the notion of love at first sight, Shae had to admit she was in way too deep already, and they'd barely met.

Why she seemed so drawn to Mason was beyond her, but she had to shake the feelings away. Far, far away, and not just because he was now her employee.

Giving up on getting any real sleep, Shae crawled from her bed at 5am on a mission for a shower and a strong cup of coffee.

One single flip of the light switch derailed her plan.

"You've got to be kidding me."

A shiver ran up Shae's spine. The house was a little colder than usual. How the hell did she not notice the power had gone out?

Because you were too busy daydreaming about a certain single dad, her brain scolded.

Her new hire! Oh god. Talk about first impressions. Was his power out too? And the baby!

Shae fumbled her way around the room, throwing on some warm clothes that she hoped somehow matched reasonably. She would need to get down to the Inn quickly, too, and check in on things. What if her guests were without power too?

Her cell phone lit up on the nightstand.

Mason Carmichael flashed on the screen.

"Hi, Mason. Are you without power too?"

"Afraid I am. I hope I didn't wake you, but I thought you should know."

"Nope, you didn't wake me. I was getting ready to head down to the Inn to check in on things there."

Mason chuckled, the sound vibrating all the way to her core. "I'm guessing you haven't looked outside yet."

"I haven't," she said as she pulled back her bedroom curtains. "Holy..."

"Surprise," he chuckled again. "I think the weather reports underestimated this storm."

"I'll say. Looks like I'll be walking to work today in my fishing waders."

"You have fishing waders?"

It was Shae's turn to laugh. "I do. Though I have to admit it will be the first time that I've worn them in the snow."

"Nice. No need for that, though. Not to sound like one of those meathead dudes, but my truck can get through this mess. Give me some time to get Thomas dressed and fed, then we'll be happy to drive you down."

"That's...you don't...." Shae wanted to refuse. Another look at the snow made her think twice. "I would appreciate that."

Another call beeped through on her phone.

"Mason, I've got another call I need to take. Is twenty minutes enough time for you to be ready?"

"I'll see you in twenty," he answered.

Shae thanked him one more time then switched over to the other call. "This is Shae."

"Morning, sleepyhead," Quinn sing-songed in her ear.

"Goodness, how are you even awake this early?" Shae teased. Knowing Quinn had been out the night before, Shae really didn't expect to hear from her this early in the morning.

"It was an early night. Listen, the main roads aren't plowed, so I'm afraid I won't make it in until later."

"Right, of course. It's totally fine. I'm heading down to the main house in a few minutes. We'll manage. Don't risk it. We'll see you when we see you."

They hung up the phone, and Shae flipped on the flashlight on her phone long enough to make sure she was presentable. Thankfully, what she'd managed to piece together in the dark looked halfway decent.

She piled her hair up in a messy bun on the top of her head, and she used a wet makeup wipe to freshen up her face before brushing her teeth with the cold water.

By the time she bundled up and made it outside, Mason was waiting for her with his truck idling on the road.

"Morning," he flashed her a grin that even in the arctic air managed to warm her insides. "I've got hot coffee in the truck and some powdered creamer and sweetener," he added as he offered a hand to help her down her porch steps and onto her shoveled sidewalk.

"How did…" she started.

"I've been up for a little bit. I think my internal clock is way off," he chuckled.

With his help, Shae climbed into the passenger side of his truck. Thomas was awake and pleasantly cooing in the backseat. "Well, good morning to you too, little dude," she smiled to herself.

"The kid is a morning person like his dad," Mason beamed with pride.

"Seems like it," Shae nodded. "A heck of a welcome from Mother Nature, huh?"

"Not much worse than Chicago," Mason shrugged. "Looks like it's going to be a white Christmas, though."

Shae let out a very unladylike snort, "You've got that right."

"Weather report says more is supposed to be coming too," Mason added.

"That sounds great," she grumbled, trying to mentally prepare herself for the chaos that she might find when they reached the Inn. Winters in Lancaster could be unpredictable. One of the only things that she loathed from time to time.

Mason took his time and made sure she arrived safely, stopping as close to the front door as possible. She half expected him to help her out of the truck then leave. Instead, he reached over and grabbed her hand, catching her by surprise and sending a tingle over her skin.

"Wait," Mason pulled his hand away like he'd been burned. Shae knew he felt it too. "I put the shovel in the back of the truck. Don't get out yet; I'll clear the walkway."

"You don't have to," Shae pointed to the ridiculous waders she had on.

"Are you always stubborn?" The question rolled off of his tongue before he even had a second to filter it. He cursed under his breath. "Sorry." He barely knew the woman, and yet he had a growing suspicion that she was as hard headed as they came.

Shae threw her head back and laughed. "If you think this is stubborn, you haven't seen anything yet."

"Well, I do believe you hired me to do a job. And while I may not be on the clock yet, I do pride myself on not being a complete asshole in general, so do me a favor and sit your pretty little behind in that seat until I've cleared the walkway off. I'd appreciate it."

Filter. Broken. That much was clear. Mason would

never speak to his employer like that. Yet, Shae managed to bring it out of him quickly.

"Message received," she rolled her eyes as Mason climbed down from his oversized truck.

While she waited in the warm cab of the truck, she mentally took stock of the property. It was clear the electricity was out here too, but thankfully it appeared the generator kicked on and the emergency lights were working. That was something to be thankful for.

Mason finished the walkway in record time then opened her door to help her down. "Can I leave my truck parked here for a little bit? I'll come inside and get started on that paperwork when you're ready, then we can talk about your snow removal plan."

Shae raised a brow.

"Woman," he warned.

"I'm stubborn; you're persistent," she said while taking his hand and trying to gracefully slide out of his truck. "You're fine here for a bit. No one is coming or going for a while."

"Good," he replied and waited until she was safely inside to head around the truck to turn it off and gather up Thomas.

A bubbly redhead with a pixie cut greeted him in the dimly lit room when he stepped inside. "Oh my gosh! You must be Mason, and this little guy must be Thomas!" The woman practically squealed.

Things looked a little different this morning, with only a few scattered lights running from what he assumed was an emergency generator. Somehow the place still maintained its holiday cheer.

"Can I hold him?" the stranger asked.

"Uhm," Mason hesitated. Funny how he had no

problem letting Shae carry him inside last night, but now he felt uncertain about anyone else holding his son.

"Oh, heavens. I've forgotten my manners," she smacked her forehead. "Mason, I'm Isla. I'm one of the hostesses here so we'll be seeing a lot of each other. Please forgive me. I love babies and apparently can't contain myself."

"Isla," he held out a hand. "Nice to meet you."

"I'm really sorry about practically attacking you and the little one," she apologized.

Mason gave her a friendly smile. "No worries. He can be a little standoffish around women."

Like his father, Mason added.

Unless the said woman was Shae.

"You know, I bet if you asked, Shae would let Thomas hang out here. Or come to work with you whenever. We'd love having the little guy around." Isla added.

Shae paused at the end of the hallway, still out of sight. She heard what Isla had said and wanted to see what Mason's reaction would be.

"I appreciate the offer, but we've already got a nanny lined up after the holidays."

Shae's heart sank a little, and she could feel an overwhelming sense of protectiveness wash over her. The thought of Thomas being left with what Shae assumed was a stranger, tore at her heartstrings.

Stepping out into the pseudo-lobby, that was more like a living room, Shae cleared her throat. She wasn't prepared to find Thomas strapped to the front of Mason's chest. Christ on a cracker that was the hottest thing she'd ever seen. And probably exactly why she opened her mouth and said, "Isla's right, I think we could probably work something out. As long as we don't actually put Thomas to work, child labor laws and all that," Shae teased, hoping it broke the awkward tension she currently felt.

What the hell was she thinking?

Mason just smirked. "We'll see about that. Is that my paperwork?" he nodded toward the stack of papers in Shae's hand.

"It is. My office isn't on the generator, so I've got no lights. You can work on these in the kitchen while I whip up breakfast in case you have any questions," she answered.

"Yeah, sure," Mason followed behind her, Thomas still cuddled against his chest.

Shae prepped the kitchen, Mason unlayered himself, and Thomas then put his son back in the carrier, where he drifted off to sleep while he worked on the paperwork. It was all fairly straightforward, but he was surprised to see something about a hiring bonus on his compensation letter.

"Uh, Shae, what's this?" he held up the paper.

She turned around from where she was whipping up eggs for the breakfast buffet. Madison and Bianca wouldn't be in today either, thanks to the two feet of snow on the ground. She didn't even need to read over what he had in his hand. Shae knew good and well what he was talking about.

Sure, the job listing didn't mention anything about a hiring bonus, but Shae felt compelled to add one especially given the fact that Mason had already proved to be the kind of guy who jumped in feet first. A little something extra in time for Christmas never hurt anyone.

Shae shrugged, "It says it's a hiring bonus. Call it whatever you want. Everyone got a bonus this year, and since you'll be official once you've signed everything, I added one for you too."

"I..."

Shae held up a hand. "Stubborn, remember? Please don't argue with me about it."

He fought off his pride and the offended feeling creeping up on him. Did Shae think he was a charity case? "You don't have to...."

"Mason, I don't do anything I don't want to do. The sooner you learn that, the better off you'll be around here. The Christmas Inn has a legacy, traditions, and a long line of integrity. We take care of our own. Like I said – every employee got a bonus this year. You've been here less than 24 hours, and you've already proven you're a go-getter and problem solver. My goal is to ensure each employee knows their worth around here."

Well, when she put it like that...

"Okay. Okay. Forget I asked," he held up his hands in surrender.

Shae went back to what she was doing, and Mason signed his name one more time. He straightened out the stack and clipped them back together before standing and stretching.

"All right, Shae. How can I help you out right now?"

"If you can get the fireplace going in the dining room," Shae pointed to a room off of the kitchen, that would be great."

"On it," he nodded.

Before he stepped out, Isla poked her head in, "I pulled one of the portable cribs out and freshened it up in case you needed to lay him down somewhere," she whispered when she noticed Thomas was already asleep.

"Oh. Wow. Okay, thank you."

"Hey, Isla, why don't you push the crib into the dining room for him? He'll be in there working for a few minutes anyway," Shae suggested.

Isla nodded and off she went while Mason relocated to the dining room.

With Thomas cuddled up in the portable crib nearby, Mason added logs to the fireplace and got a fire burning with ease.

Shae joined him a few minutes later, pushing a cart with buffet trays piled on top.

Mason helped her set-up the breakfast buffet then joined her for a bite to eat, at her insistence, before the Inn's guests stirred and gathered in the dining room.

CHAPTER 7

Five hundred miles away in the snow-covered mountains of Tennessee, Garland and Debby Tinsley nestled together in front of the fireplace. Holding hands and watching the flames dance, they soaked in a moment of rest after a long day's work.

In the corner of their living room, the star on top of the Christmas tree blinked.

"It's happening," Debby whispered.

Garland nodded. "I know, dear." He patted her leg and smiled.

It was a tale as old as time.

The sheer magic of Christmas.

As pure as the white snow falling on the ground.

The dreams returned, foretelling a future of love. Filled with laughter and happiness.

"He'll be good for her."

"And she'll heal him." Garland agreed.

AFTER BREAKFAST MASON FOUND HIS WAY TO AN old barn on the property where the tractor and a bunch of other equipment was stored. From there he plowed the property and even went over to the adjoining farm to clear out some snow for Jerimiah and his wife for Shae. Then he jumped on whatever else he could possibly help Shae with.

Getting to work with Thomas was an adventure in itself.

Isla and Shae fawned over his son while he alternated working with Thomas strapped to his chest, napping in the portable crib, or entertaining the ladies inside.

It made for one hell of an interesting day. And if he was being honest, he was exhausted but the good kind of exhaustion that came from a hard day's work. Something he found he had indeed been missing.

With most of the snow cleared on the property and a few main roads finally opening back up, some of the guests were able to check out and head back home as they planned. While other guests who planned to stay through Christmas decided that even with the power not being restored, they were more than happy to stay and enjoy a bit of old fashion coziness.

Turned out – losing power didn't damper The Christmas Inn's holiday spirit at all. Guests made the best of it with a bit of help from Isla, and Shae improvised and adapted to keep the itinerary as close to normal for everyone as possible.

He even joined *everyone* for dinner in the dining room. A dinner that he was surprised to find two of the female guests helping Shae with. Together they'd prepared quite a feast that Mason graciously insisted on helping clean up. All while Isla ran off with Thomas, who surprisingly decided the woman with red hair and Christmas tree earrings was his new best friend.

That's how he ended up back in the kitchen all alone with Shae.

Shae, who was hand washing dishes while swaying her

hips and singing along to Christmas Carols that played on her phone.

Mason fought back a groan every time he almost bumped into her while cleaning up.

Not even his ex had this kind of effect on him.

Christ, he could swear the temperature in the kitchen was rising.

He ran a hand over his face. He needed to get it together. No amount of celibacy was an excuse to make a move on Shae. Besides, a woman like Shae probably believed in happily ever after and fairytales. Mason swore those things off when his ex broke his heart and dumped their son on his doorstep. He didn't have time for flings or relationships when he had Thomas to worry about.

"You're thinking awful loudly over there. Are you okay? Please tell me we haven't scared you off already, and you're thinking about running away," Shae startled him.

"What? No. A little hard work isn't going to drive me away."

"Good," she patted his chest without thinking.

That was a bad idea. A horrible idea. For one, she could feel his heart racing under that stupid plaid shirt he was wearing, not to mention his hard pecs.

"Now, who's lost in their own head?" he quirked a brow.

"Right. Sorry about that."

"About?" Mason asked.

"That," Shae waved her hand around. "Patting your chest like some weirdo. I should keep my hands to myself before you come at me for unprofessional conduct."

"This isn't football, Shae," he chuckled.

"No, but there's a whole policy about employee treatment."

Fuck. Mason hissed and swallowed hard. Why the hell did he want to kiss her so badly? "What if the employee consented?"

What? His brain must have short-circuited. He was toeing a fragile line and about to blow it all.

"Well, that would be different. As long as both parties agreed."

Mason stepped a little closer to her. "Would you agree?"

"Agree to what exactly?" Shae couldn't think clearly with Mason this close to her. Not with his intoxicating scent lingering around them. Not with his lips mere inches from hers and every cell in her body short circuiting.

"I haven't a goddamn clue, Shae. A kiss? Something. There's this goddamn pull; it's dragging me in, and damn if I can control it. I felt it the moment I stepped foot inside that door last night."

Even with a million reasons why *not* running through his head, he felt like his heart was screaming *yes!*

He could ignore it all. He should. Turn and walk away. Go home for the night. Clearly, he was suffering from exhaustion. That's it. A good night's rest, and he'd wake with a clear head. Or maybe he was caught up in a dream right now.

Shae moved forward.

Nope. Not a dream. Both of her hands were on his chest now. "I feel it too," she whispered. "It was like my heart knew who you were the minute I saw you. Fucking Tinsley Christmas curse." The last sentence came out more like a mutter.

"What was that?"

"The Tinsley Christmas curse. I supposed it's not actually a curse, depending on how you look at it, but...there's this whole thing. Started with my grandparents. Something about Christmas Magic and falling in love. The Christmas Inn is said to attract matching hearts. I've never understood it."

Mason brushed a loose strand of blonde hair behind her ear. "Do you believe in it?"

Wouldn't it figure? Christmas Magic. Here he moved across the country for a new beginning and a place of joy to raise his son, and in an instant, he found himself falling for Shae. It was almost comical. Hell, it would have been if not for the hard-on confined by denim and begging to be set free right along with his heart that felt like it was walking outside his chest.

"I thought it was just a coincidence. But first Isla, then Quinn, now here we are," her voice hitched.

"I'll be damned. Might explain why a random job listing ended up on my screen when I originally had no plans of moving away from Chicago," Mason confessed.

So. Close. He was so close that he almost pressed his lips to hers.

A loud hum and the sound of the entire building sparking to life caught them both by surprise, along with the sound of a text from Shae's phone.

"I should check that," she stepped back quickly. The moment was completely broken now.

Nana: You found him! Oh, my sweet girl. You've met the one! I just know it.

Shae gasped. No. There was no way.

How would Nana know anything about what was happening here from all the way in Tennessee?

Nana: It's a Christmas Inn Miracle. I've been dreaming about this day for weeks now.

Her grandmother went on to describe Mason, and Thomas, in great detail.

Quinn. It had to be Quinn. This was a joke. Quinn was in on it and called Nana. That would explain it all. There was no other way her grandmother would know what Mason looked like or that he had a child.

Nana: Don't fight it. Believe in magic.

Shae's heart beat faster. Believe in magic. Wasn't that exactly what she heard in her mind when Mason walked through the door last night? That exact phrase she heard when she went running from his house because something felt...right.

"I should go," Mason backed up toward the door. "With the power back on, I should go check on my place and get Thomas settled for the night. It's been a long day."

"Mason, wait," she called out.

He shook his head. "No, really. I need to get Thomas home and ready for bed before his whole schedule is thrown off, and he refuses to go to sleep tonight."

Could she really let him walk away from her like that?

"But..."

"Unless you need me before then, I'll see you after Christmas."

His "official" start date. Right.

Mason turned around and vanished down the hall.

What the hell just happened?

One minute they were as close as two people could physically be. Now she felt like someone dumped a bucket of ice over her head.

Mason gathered Thomas and said goodbye to Isla.

Tinsley Christmas curse? The legend of The Christmas Inn?

There was no way any of that was true. Or was it?

Could he have really met his true love? Hell, did he even believe in love at first sight? Lust? Hell yes, he'd felt lust at first sight more than once. This was different, though.

There was a deep primal need. A connection that he couldn't make sense of. And if he was being honest, he felt it the moment he saw the job listing. He couldn't explain *why* it felt so right.

Maybe there was some truth to the whole falling in love "story," but how the hell was Mason to know?

He tried to rationalize what Shae and told him over and over while he cleaned Thomas up and put him in his pajamas. What ran through his head as he rocked Thomas by the fire felt more like a movie playing on the Hallmark channel. He *could* see a future – a future he never expected – with Shae. It was like he just *knew* deep down in his soul what his future looked like, and The Christmas Inn was front and center in all of it.

Mason could even see a growing Thomas living his life to the fullest. Playing in the snow, chasing goats and horses. And there Thomas was, getting ready for his prom and his wedding day.

He froze then shook his head. No. That couldn't be right.

"Believe in magic." It sounded like the wind whispered.

Thomas smiled in his sleep.

He really needed to take his cues from his son and go to bed.

Slowly and carefully, he rose from the rocker and tiptoed upstairs to tuck Thomas into the crib Mason put together the night before when he couldn't sleep – and before the power went out.

Thomas rolled to his side and stuck his thumb in his mouth, staying sound asleep the whole time.

Mason crossed the hall to his room and considered

plopping face-first onto the bed to sleep, not even bothering to change his clothes. Two steps into his room, and he could have sworn he heard a knock at the door.

"Believe in magic."

Another knock.

"So much for going to bed," he grumbled to himself, then trekked back down the steps.

He could see Shae through the front window, standing on his front porch.

"Hey, come in out of the cold," he pulled open the door and moved back so she could walk in.

Shae ran her hands over her arms to warm up. "I'm really sorry to bother you. I know you said you'd see me after Christmas, and you're not on the clock, so I really should leave you to it...."

"Shae, it's not a bother. Earlier was...a lot, and I needed some space."

"Right. A lot. Kinda crazy and all that. But uhm, I actually came over because I very foolishly didn't think to leave a faucet or two running while the power was out, and well, now my place is flooded and frozen. I would have just gone back to the Inn, but Quinn could finally make it in, and she brought Madison, one of my cooks. They both took the only left-over room and," she swallowed back a sob. She was not going to cry. A minor flood and icicles hanging from her ceiling would not ruin her.

"You need a place to stay," Mason finished without hesitation.

"Y-y-yes."

He nodded. "Say no more. You can take the master, and I'll sleep across the hall with Thomas."

Shae looked down at her feet. "Could we, maybe, talk a little more first?"

Mason tilted her chin up with the tip of his finger and smirked, "About magic?"

With Shae looking right at him, he noticed her eyes twinkle for the first time. "I know it sounds farfetched, but if we...."

"Just believe?" Mason finished.

Shae gasped. "Have you, uhm, heard that before? Like, maybe, recently?"

"Twice. Tonight. Once was right before you knocked on my door."

"And?"

"I believe. Especially after what happened when I was rocking Thomas to sleep."

Shae heard the stories her whole life. Stories of how generations of Tinsley's met their soulmates and fell in love. All at the Original Christmas Inn in Tennessee.

She *never* thought that miles away, in a brand-new location, love would find her.

Yet, her heart knew, and if the look on Mason's face was anything to go on, his heart knew it too.

"It's unexplainable, isn't it?" he asked, his arms still resting on her shoulders just inside his front door.

"In reality? Yeah. It is. It's like a fairytale that you might read about as a child, and the same fairytale that you realize as an adult doesn't exist."

"Except it does. Otherwise, I don't think I'd be standing here now. I mean, Shae – there's a Christmas Inn *in* Chicago, and I never knew it existed until I saw your job listing. On a search for jobs still in the Chicago area. None of my Christmas memories have been pleasant, and yet, I knew this was the place I needed to raise Thomas. Then, while I was rocking him, I could see it all in complete clarity."

"Like a movie on a movie screen?" Shae asked.

"Exactly like that."

"Hm," her voice dropped. "Then, what happens next?"

"That depends on how much trouble I'll be in if I kiss you."

"I think you'll be in more trouble if you don't kiss me because the truth is, I've been on the verge of combusting from the moment I saw you."

Mason cleared his throat. "Shae, if I start kissing you now, I don't know that I'll ever be able to stop."

"Then, I guess it's a damn good thing fate is giving us a lifetime."

CHAPTER 8

When Mason said he'd never be able to stop, he wasn't lying.

His lips pressed to Shae's and before she knew it, she was flat on her back on the couch. Mason hovered over her while worshiping her from head to toe. Her coat was discarded somewhere along with the heavy sweater she'd thrown on earlier that morning and her pants were currently being drug down her legs.

Mason was like a man starved and Shae was more than happy to be feasted on but when his tongue danced along the sensitive flesh between her legs she could have sworn she had died and gone to heaven. She fought the urge to clamp her thighs closed, to cover herself up and hide from the beautiful man who touched not only her heart but her soul as well. Then he had to go and add his fingers to the mix, sending her soaring.

Her own fingers tangled in his hair as her hips rose off the sofa and Mason's name tumbled from her lips.

Shae found herself filled with an unfamiliar need. A need for so much more from the man before her. She needed Mason almost as much as she needed her next breath. Yes, it was sudden and unexpected; and she wanted to fight whatever it was that happened – that was happening between them. But the truth of the matter was that deep down, Shae *did* believe in magic. She believed in the family traditions and the Christmas Magic that floated around this place, *her* place. It wasn't just in the walls of The Christmas Inn. It was in her heart, her bloodline.

She knew with every fiber of her being that she had met her match. Her soulmate. And nothing would be able to stand between them.

Well except for the latex condom that Mason was currently rolling over his impressive length.

Shae swallowed back a groan and flexed her hips again. "Yes. Yes, please," she begged.

Mason pressed against her wet entrance then blew out a breath as he paused. "We're doing this. It's happening."

She couldn't tell if he was reassuring her or himself. "Oh, it's happening. I'm right here in the moment with you, Mason."

"This isn't me. I don't make a habit of doing these sorts of things with women I've just met."

And yet here he was with a woman he felt like he had known his entire life about to make love to her. A woman that he only truly knew for twenty-four hours but had somehow fallen madly in love with. The same woman that he felt a connection so deep that he wholeheartedly believed he'd found his forever.

"You're mine, Shae. This changes everything and the minute I've claimed you...you. Are. Mine."

"I'm yours," she whispered, framing his face with her hands, and pulling him in closer to kiss him. "Take me, Mason. Claim me, forever."

When she put it like that, Mason found it hard to resist. Sliding his cock inside her, he let out a groan. The sensation was overwhelming. It may sound stupid, cliché even but the feeling between them right now was unexplainable. It felt so right, and so unforgettably different. For the first time in his life, he was beginning to understand the difference in intimacy with someone you love and simply having sex to fulfill a physical need. There was a connection that ran so deep with Shae.

"Goddamn," he hissed. "Shae."

"I know," she wrapped her legs around him and lifted her hips to draw him in even more.

"This is…"

"Everything," Shae finished for him.

Three little words danced on the edge of his tongue. He expected warning bells to ring in his head or his internal filter to shut down all thoughts of one four letter word. When that didn't happen, Mason nearly let them slip.

Shae reaching up to pinch her own nipples sidetracked him into silence while his pace quickened. The woman was absolute perfection. Unafraid to take the lead or tell him what she wanted, with or without words.

Her back arched and her eyes snapped closed as Mason ran his thumb over her clit. He could feel her walls tightening around him. She was close. So close.

"Look at me, Shae."

Her eyes opened and locked on his.

"Trust me?"

"Completely."

Mason slid his free hand up her torso and wrapped it loosely around her neck. Her eyes widened in shock and her core tightened. "Still good," he panted between thrusts.

"Yes," she shuddered.

"Good," he smirked, squeezing his hand around her only a little bit more to heighten her pleasure. It was a trick he learned a long time ago and somehow he knew she'd appreciate it. He thrusted deeper and harder until she was shaking in pleasure then he released his hand and draped both of her legs over his shoulders.

Shae cursed as stars filled her vision. Whatever voodoo magic Mason performed was better than fireworks on the 4th of July and damn it, she wanted more. "Mason!" she cried out just as he began to explode.

His own body quivered, and he let out a primal growl that turned Shae on even more. When he stilled and dropped his forehead to hers she sighed contently.

She wanted to wrap her arms around him and bury her face in the crock of his neck while drifting off to the kind of peaceful sleep that only came with post-coital bliss.

A tiny cry from upstairs quickly pulled them both from the bubble they'd just be lost in.

Mason muttered a curse as he slid out of her and peeled off the condom. He picked up his boxers from somewhere in the frenzied piles of clothes and pulled them on, then rushed into the kitchen to toss the condom and wash his hands before running up the stairs with a baby bottle in hand.

Shae slowly sat up on the couch and put her head in her hands.

What the hell just happened? *You had the most mind-blowing sex – ever. With your brand new employee!* Her brain shouted. *And you loved every damn minute of it.*

One thing was certain, that old family Christmas Magic tale never mentioned anything about...that.

Shudders. And why would it?

This wasn't like Shae. She didn't make a habit of sleeping with men she barely knew. And hadn't she sworn off the notion of relationships until she had a better handle on the inn?

A chill breezed over her and she let out a snort, realizing

that she was still stark naked on this man's living room couch. She needed to put her clothes back on. Quickly, in case he brought that adorable baby down the steps. That was the very last thing she needed. Then once she was dressed Shae could try to figure out what to do next.

Why? Why did her own house have to be flooded right now? What she wanted to do was run away and hide just like she did the night before when things felt all too real for her.

Yet what sounded like her grandmother's voice ringing in her ear, reminded her to believe in magic once more.

CHAPTER 9

Mason rocked Thomas in his arms while the little guy downed his bottle and drifted back to sleep.

His mind was elsewhere though. Mainly on the woman downstairs. And this whole notion of Christmas Magic and the allegedly Tinsley Christmas "Curse" as Shae put it.

He had sex with his boss. Enjoyed the hell out of it. And would do it again. In a heartbeat.

Was he really ready for a relationship though? Not that sex meant forever but something told Mason that in this case - it did.

Thomas finished his bottle and burped for Mason without waking up. He laid his son back in his crib and patted his back until he was sure Thomas was out like a light then he tiptoed out of the room.

Pausing at the top of the stairs, he blew out a breath before he made his way back to the beautiful woman who was hopefully still waiting for him.

And waiting for him she was. With a mug of hot cocoa in her hand.

"I hope you don't mind that I helped myself. I made you a cup too," she pointed to a mug on the counter. "It's one of my vices, next to a damn good cup of coffee."

Mason picked up the cup and took a sip. "I don't mind at all. Thanks for making me a cup, too." This...it all felt familiar. So familiar in fact that he had to resist the urge to pull her close and kiss her cheek like they'd done this a thousand times before.

"Thomas went back to sleep okay?"

He nodded. "Yeah, he did. He's a fairly decent sleeper as long as his whole bedtime routine happens."

"You seem to have this whole parenting thing under control."

To that, Mason laughed. "I really don't. I'm kinda flying by the seat of my pants really."

"Can I ask...about his mom? You mentioned no wife. What's the story there?"

How many times had he avoided that question back in Chicago? Changed the subject and refused to talk about it. Yet, he felt safe telling Shae about it.

"The short version is that his mom is my ex-fiancée. She left and didn't bother to tell me she was pregnant. Showed up on my doorstep one night with Thomas in her arms. Handed him off and never looked back. It's been me and him ever since."

Shae's eyes widened in shock. "That's...I...I'm so sorry. I can't imagine abandoning my child like that."

"Honestly, I can't either. I called in a few favors, took a DNA test and my lawyer took care of the rest."

"He's lucky to have you."

"Nah. I think I'm the lucky one." And he meant it. In fact, if not for Thomas he probably would have never met Shae.

"Sooooooo, uhm...I should probably get some rest," she finished her hot chocolate and moved to put the mug in the sink.

Mason reached for her arm. "We should probably talk

first. You know, about what happened. Where we go from here."

Shae sighed. "I was afraid you'd say that."

"I don't want to screw this up. I've got Thomas to think about and I can't risk losing this job either," he told her.

"I get that. No matter what, Mason, your job is safe. I'm not that type of person that would fire you or make you miserable for personal reasons."

He smirked. "I didn't think you were."

"As for this," she pointed between the two of them. "Call me crazy, but I want to see where this goes. I think we'd be foolish not to."

"Yeah. I'd like that, too," he kissed her lips. "You should know, I don't do casual though."

"I don't do relationships in general. At least I swore I didn't. Until you," Shae chuckled.

On that they could agree on.

"Come to bed with me?"

"You think that's a good idea?"

Mason shrugged. "After what happened here tonight, why the hell not?"

He was throwing caution to the wind on this one, but wasn't that exactly what he'd been doing since he applied for a job on the other side of the country?

"Morning comes early, can you promise to keep your hands to yourself?"

He answered by swooping her up in his arms and carrying her up the steps.

"I think the better question is, can you be quiet?" he growled as he gently shut his bedroom door.

Shae woke up to a slight chill in the air and an empty bed. Her clothes were still discarded all over Mason's bedroom floor but she quickly found a t-shirt long enough to cover all of the important pieces so she could tiptoe to the bathroom down the hall.

The smell of cinnamon and peppermint waffled through the early morning air along with the sound of Mason's voice making small talk with Thomas.

An old familiar feeling rested in Shae's heart.

Home.

Childhood memories and a clear picture of her future. A future that included a little brown haired boy and a girl with little blonde curls.

Shae gasped and held on tightly to the bathroom sink as pictures of a future swept through her.

Was that the same thing Mason had seen the night before?

The way she saw it, she had two choices. She could run and never look back or she could walk down those steps and embrace what the future held for them. And, well, Shae was never the one to run away.

She splashed a little water on her face and stood tall as she walked out of the bathroom and tiptoed down the steps.

Mason moved around the kitchen in a pair of flannel pajama pants, cooking up breakfast and entertaining Thomas who was on the counter in his bouncy seat. It was a sight to behold and one that would stay itched in Shae's mind forever.

"Hey, you're up early," Mason grinned, the moment he noticed her watching.

"Some of us have to work today," she teased.

"Well, lucky for you, you can start the day with a hot cup of coffee and a full belly," he said as he slid a plate filled with food onto the table.

Shae moved closer to him. "I, can I…"

Mason seemed to read her mind. "After last night, I think we're past formalities and asking permission to give affection," he said, pulling her in and giving her a hug and a kiss on the cheek. "Morning."

She blushed. "Morning. And thank you for breakfast."

"Of course, I wouldn't be able to do all of this without an angel who stocked the whole place."

"That was nothing," she brushed off his comment.

He finished making his own plate and joined her at the small table to eat while Thomas seemed content bouncing around as long as he had eyes on his father.

"I'm going to have to find a plumber and maybe a general contractor for my place today," Sadie sighed.

"You can stay here as long as you want," Mason said without hesitation.

"I appreciate that but I usually keep an empty room down at the main house for staff emergencies. I can just stay there."

"Okay. What if I wanted you to stay here?"

Sadie paused. "Well, I'd say that it seems a little soon."

"It does. But, I don't think anything about the two of us has gone by the book. Wouldn't you agree?"

"I snore," Shae threw out there.

"And I sometimes leave dirty clothes on the floor. I do my own laundry though."

"What kind of example would we be setting for Thomas?" Shae questioned.

Mason chuckled. "I think we would be teaching him that life is sometimes unexplainable and you should never hesitate to take the chance. And that he should believe in magic."

"You seem to have this all figured out."

"I don't have any of this figured out," he shook his head. "But something about this feels right, so, I'm trusting it."

"Fine. I'll stay here. Until everything is fixed at my place and then we'll revisit it."

"Fair enough."

CHAPTER 10

ONE YEAR LATER...

In true Christmas Inn fashion, the pine tree garden was decorated from top to bottom. Ornaments, garland, and ribbons of green, red, sliver, and gold, twinkled from the carefully strung lights on the trees and entwined with the fresh garland wrapped around the archway Mason stood under.

The temperature was a little colder than he would have preferred for an outdoor wedding, but it was what Shae wanted. And well, he'd do anything for the woman who captured his heart a year ago. The large space heaters carefully placed around the garden and near the makeshift altar helped keep the chill from being unbearable.

Still, their adorable ring bearer was bundled up from head to toe in an all-black snowsuit and tucked into the little red wagon with a blanket. Mason still couldn't believe how different his life was a year ago. If not for his son, Mason may have never moved to Lancaster. Funny how fate worked in their favor.

The bridal march began to play. Mason anxiously adjusted his tie and stood up a little straighter as the garden gates opened. A breath hitched in his throat as his beautiful bride came into view.

There she was. In a long sleeved snow-white gown with

a faux fur shawl over her shoulders, Shae looked like an angel.

His angel.

Dominic clapped him on the back. "She's pretty as a picture, man."

"Breathtaking," he replied.

Guests stood as she began walking down the aisle, escorted by her father and grandfather. When she reached the end of the aisle, Mason stepped forward to meet them. Both men kissed her cheeks then handed her off to Mason.

"Hi," she whispered.

"Hi yourself," he smiled back at her with tear filled eyes. Today was absolutely one of the happiest days of his life.

He had no idea when he decided on a whim to move across the country that he would be standing here a year later, marrying the woman who literally took his breath away.

"Dearly beloved, we are gathered here today..." the minister began to speak.

Lost in Shae's eyes, everything else faded into the background. He barely heard anything that was said. Until it was time to exchange vows.

In front of their family and friends they exchanged promises of love, laughter, health and happiness. Then it was time for him to kiss his bride.

Like a man that had gone without for too long – and he had been since Shae insisted on a few traditions, including not spending the night before the wedding together – he cupped her face in his hands and pressed his lips to hers. If not for the guests joining them, he would have gladly stayed right there in that moment with her forever.

A few whoops and hollers from their guests, egged on

by Dom and Callen of course, pulled the two love birds apart.

"I love you Mrs. Carmichael," Mason whispered only for her to hear as snowflakes began to fall from the sky.

It was kismet. After all, it was snow that forced them together in the most unexpected way.

"I love you too, Husband."

The grin on Mason's face grew bigger and he shook his head in disbelief. "I don't think I'll ever get tired of hearing that."

As the minister introduced them for the first time as Mr. and Mrs. - Mason looped her arm in his and squeezed her hand. "What do you say we take this somewhere warmer?" he grinned like a fool.

Shae tried to hide her shiver and laughed. "Yes, please."

Hand in hand they walked down the aisle past their guests and into the warmth of the bridal suite.

"I can't believe we're married," Shae leaned her head onto his shoulder and sighed.

"How long do we have before we have to join our guests?" Mason asked with a wiggle of his eyebrows.

"Not nearly long enough for all the things I want to do with my husband," Shae licked her lips, eliciting a groan from Mason.

"We are the guests of honor, they can wait," he said, giving her hips a squeeze. What he wouldn't give to slide his hands under the lace and tulle of her dress to see if she was wearing panties or if she carried through with the threat to go without.

Fuck waiting. He needed to know. And he wanted to give her part of her wedding gift.

Mason flipped the lock on the door. "I'm not going to

make it another four hours if I don't at least have a taste," he growled before backing her up to the couch.

Shae lost her balance and flopped backwards onto the plush cushions with a laugh.

That laughter died quickly on her lips when Mason knelt at her feet and pushed her legs apart.

"Oh," she gasped as his fingers danced up her legs, taking the fabric of her wedding dress with him.

"Mmmm, someone kept their promise," he hummed in delight. Shae was bare for him.

Mason took his time nipping and teasing her before he finally swiped his tongue across her sensitive nub. Shae's hips lifted off the sofa and she practically purred.

"Mason!" she gasped.

"Shh, wouldn't want our guests to hear you," he smirked between her legs.

The thrill of knowing that there was an entire room full of wedding guests just on the other side of the door had Shae's core clenching around his fingers.

He continued on with his mission until Shae was near her peak, then he retreated with a wicked grin.

"Really," Shae arched her brow.

Mason licked his lips and pulled the little surprise from his pocket.

"Uhm."

He winked and flicked a button setting the silicone toy buzzing.

"You wouldn't," Shae gulped.

His answer was to simply rub the egg-shaped vibrator against her clit. A string of curses flew from her lips as Mason swirled it in different directions before slipping it inside her. He let her have the first orgasm with the vibrator tucked inside her pussy while his tongue flicked her clit but that was all she wouldn't be getting right now.

Once she settled Mason shut the vibrator off, pocketed the remote and smoothed Shae's wedding dress back into place.

"Wait!" she gasped.

Mason pretended he didn't know what she was about to say as he took her hand and tugged her back on her feet.

"Mason. I can't."

This time he pressed a button that had her clenching her thighs.

"Fuck," she squealed, squeezing his arm as if that would stop him.

"There will be plenty of time for that later," he fought back a grin. "If I have to make it through the next four hours knowing you're bare under that dress, then consider this your punishment."

"I can't go out there..." her words were cut off with another pulse of vibrations. "Mason!"

Oh, he was going to have a whole lot of fun with this.

"How am I going to..." another flick of a button.

"Goddamnit, Mason. I can't go there with you doing..." she squirmed. "THAT!"

"You'll be fine," he wrapped his arms around her and kissed her, "wifey."

"One rule, please," she pleaded.

"I'm listening."

"Do not turn that damn thing on while I'm dancing with my father."

Mason scoffed. "I'm a lot of things but I am not a complete pig."

He turned it on one more time for good measure.

"I will get you back for this," she promised.

"Not only am I going to hold you to that, I'm looking forward to it Mrs. Carmichael."

That wasn't the only thing he was looking forward to. There was an entire lifetime ahead of them that he couldn't wait to start.

"Now, let's go dance the night away."

THEIR OFFICIAL INTRODUCTION OUT OF THE WAY, Mason and Shae made their way around the room to greet all their guests.

When they reached the table where their work family sat, Shae's previous groundskeeper glowed next to his wife. "Mason, I don't think you actually had the pleasure of meeting Fletcher."

Mason extended his hand and introduced himself.

"And this is my gorgeous wife, Dorothea," Fletcher grinned.

"Dorothea," Mason kissed the back of her hand. "We're all glad you're here."

That was more than an understatement.

"You're feeling well?" Shae asked with a hint of concern.

"Better than ever," Dorothea nodded. "It's truly a miracle."

Looking at the woman now, no one would ever know that Dorothea was diagnosed with an aggressive cancer a year ago. Fletcher quit because doctors warned that Dorothea's time was limited. Now, they were calling it a miracle. Her scans came back clean and there was no sign of the cancer that threatened to kill her.

Nothing could convince Shae that it wasn't that very same magic that had touched their lives too.

"Thank you both for being here," Shae said with a tearful smile.

The DJ interrupted, calling for their first dance and they happy couple excused themselves.

Mason twirled Shae around the dance floor for their first dance with a smile permanently etched on his face.

Thomas stumbled around them, still learning the whole walking thing.

Shae looked up at Mason and smiled. "I think now may be a good time to tell you that our little boy isn't going to be an only child for long."

Without skipping a beat, Mason's grin grew. "I know."

"You know?"

"A little girl, with little blonde curls just like her mom," he said, twirling a loose curl around his finger.

Shae laughed through tears of joy.

"Christmas Magic," they both sighed.

In the sea of guests, Shae's grandparents swayed arm in arm.

"Two down, three more to go." Debby winked.

Her sweet husband, Garland, chuckled. "I don't think the next one is going to be so easily convinced."

Debby huffed. "Nicole, doesn't stand a chance."

Epilogue

Twenty years later...

Shae gasped and sat up in bed. It was their 20th wedding anniversary and they decided to take a trip to the original Christmas Inn in Tennessee to celebrate, leaving their daughter Joyanna to manage things until they got home.

"Hey," Mason sat up and rubbed his eyes. "What is it?"

The star atop the Christmas tree in their room flickered.

"It's happening," Shae whispered. "Our little girl is about to fall in love."

Mason could feel it too. Just like he could when it was Thomas who fell in love. "I'm not sure how I feel about this," he chuckled.

Call it cliché or old fashioned but something was different about the thought of his little girl falling in love and starting her own family.

"Well, now you know how I felt when it was Thomas who was meeting his true love for the first time." Shae rested her head on his shoulder.

"You know, the last twenty years have been nothing but magic. And I would have never believed it until I met you," he kissed the top of her head.

Shae snickered. "I didn't believe it either. Until you."

"But, you and I both know that Joyanna hangs on every word of all those old stories."

"Oh, I know. Which means whoever this young man is..."

"In for one hell of a surprise," Mason finished.

"It still feels weird to be *here* and not home for Christmas."

Mason clicked his tongue. "Oh no you don't. You are not cutting our anniversary trip short to go home and meddle. You'll let nature happen."

"Magic. Let the magic happen," Shae poked his side.

"Nature, fate, magic. With this family it's all the same."

A crystal clear picture of Joyanna's true love hit her like a ton of bricks and Shae hissed. "I don't think you're gonna like it when you realize *who* she's about to fall for."

It wouldn't take long before Mason saw it too. Until then, Shae was going to try to enjoy the peace.

JOYANNA SAT AT THE FRONT DESK OF The Christmas Inn, reading her favorite Christmas romance and daydreaming about the day that her own prince charming would walk through the door to sweep her off her feet.

Her whole life, Joyanna had been told the story of The Christmas Inn and the Christmas Magic that lived within those walls.

She watched as her older brother Thomas came home from college for Christmas two years ago and fell in love with the daughter of one of their guests. And every year on Christmas she was subjected to the story of how her own parents met and fell in love right in this very room.

And so she waited. Wondering when it would be her turn.

The bell overtop the door jingled, pulling her from her daydreams.

"Hi, welcome to. . ." she blinked twice. "Keaton?"

No. No. No. This was not happening.

There was no way.

"Joyanna."

No. Why did his voice sound different? So, sexy and. . .no. There was no way that Keaton was *the one.*

"Thomas isn't here," she mumbled through gritted teeth.

And why did he look so damn good looking in his work uniform?

"Good thing I didn't come out here for Thomas then," he winked.

And why was he being so nice to her?

He's always been nice to you, her brain shouted.

No. No and NO. She was not falling for her brother's best friend. There was no way that Keaton was her true love.

"What can I do for you?" Joyanna tried to remain calm, in spite of the butterflies in her stomach.

"Well, there's a snowstorm coming and the heat's broken in my apartment. Landlord can't get it fixed until after the holidays. I was hoping that there might be a room available here, at the Inn."

"You want a room, here. On Christmas Eve? We're booked, and I know you know that." She scolded.

"I also know that your parents have *always* kept a spare room for family emergencies."

"And you think that as Thomas' best friend, you're family?"

"Tell me I'm not," he challenged.

"You could stay at my parents place," the words flew out of her mouth before she could stop them.

Snowed in. Until after the holidays. With Keaton.

Joyanna would never survive.

"With you?"

She meant to say - no. She meant to tell him that she would stay at the Inn and he could have the whole house to himself. Instead she said, "Is that a problem for you?"

"Never," he said with a sure smile that did things to her. Things that she had never felt before.

Then she heard it. The tell-tale sign that her parents told her about.

"Believe in Magic."

Keaton startled and looked around. "Did you hear something?"

Shit. He heard it too.

"Nope. Nothing," she lied. "I'll get you the spare key."

THE CHRISTMAS INN SERIES CONTINUES WITH Christmas Inn Blue Ridge, *coming this July!*

Also by Aubree Valentine

Too Hot to Handle Series
Hot Cop
Cop Tease
Strip Search
Cop Blocked
Covert Affair
Wild Fire
Ex-Con
Fed Up

The R&D Stables Series
Ranger

The following titles are now in Kindle Unlimited:

The Day and Knight Trio
Damon
Knight
Gigi (coming in 2023)

425 Madison Series
Love Under Construction
Love Under Protection

Susan Stoker's Badge of Honor World
Justice for Danielle
Rescuing Harlow
Saving Sadie

Man of the Month Club - Sycamore Mountain
Drunk Dial

Curves for Christmas
Sugar Cookie Kisses

The Christmas Inn Series
Christmas Inn Lancaster
Christmas Inn Blue Ridge
Christmas Inn Piegon Forge
Christmas Inn St. Petersburg

The Rexford Royals Series
Royally F*cked
Royally Scr*wed

Stay Connected

Come join my reader group on Facebook!

Stay up-to-date on new releases, information, and exclusive content. Sign up for my newsletter where you can also grab your FREE copy of *Double Shot* - a Too Hot to Handle Series Prequel.

Find me on social media:
Facebook
Tik Tok
Twitter
Instagram
Amazon
BookBub
Goodreads
Pinterest
www.authoraubreevalentine.com

About the Author

Aubree Valentine began her book world career back in 2016 as a virtual assistant for a friend/fellow author and as a book blogger. But, she began writing stories long before that. After carefully learning the ins and outs of the Indie book business, Aubree finally decided to give publishing a try for herself - with a whole lot of encouragement from the friends and mentors she met along the way.

Her first book, Take Back My Heart, was released in the fall of 2016, with its follow-up - Come Back to Me launching a year later. They were quickly followed by her breakout novel, Hot Cop, part of the Too Hot to Handle Series.

Aubree has a degree in sarcasm and resides in Pennsylvania with her husband, two children and several furbabies. She enjoys reading, chasing after her twins (or trying to keep them out of trouble), cuddling with her husband, and coming up with new project ideas that often involve power tools.

She's usually always online via Facebook or Instagram

@authoraubreevalentine or Tik Tok @aubreewritesromance .

www.authoraubreevalentine.com

Made in the USA
Middletown, DE
04 October 2023